New Friend for Nai'a

Story by Katie Grove-Velasquez

Illustrations by Michael Ogata

MUTUAL PUBLISHING

ISBN-10: 1-56647-912-6
ISBN-13: 978-1-56647-912-7

Library of Congress Catalog Card Number:

First Printing September 2009

Mutual Publishing, LLC
1215 Center Street, Suite 210
Honolulu, Hawai'i 96816
Ph: 808-732-1709 / Fax: 808-734-4094
email: info@mutualpublishing.com
www.mutualpublishing.com

Printed in Taiwan

A new bottlenose calf was traveling around the island, guided by her mother. Today was her birthday and her mother had promised her a tour of the reef. Since she was born only hours before, her mother wanted to make sure she adjusted quickly.

"Where are we going, mother?" she asked excitedly.

"We are going to meet the neighbors, dear," her mother replied. "Now you stay close to me, okay?"

"Okay." Nai`a quickened her pace to keep up with her mother.

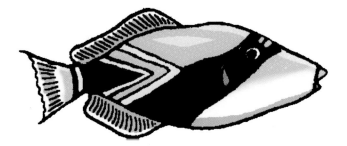

Everywhere they went Nai'a looked about with wonder. All the new faces looked friendly, and she wanted to talk with everyone. The many pretty coral reefs with their brightly colored inhabitants looked like a promising place to go exploring in the future. Nai'a felt giddy with excitement. There was so much to do and see!

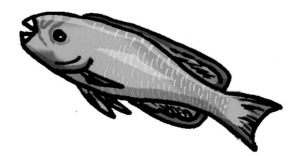

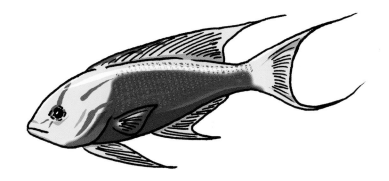

Around a corner they came upon a sleeping green sea turtle. Nai`a quickened her pace, anxious to make a new friend. "Good afternoon, Mr. Turtle. I am Nai`a and today is my birthday!" The dolphin smiled down upon the turtle.

"Your birthday, you say?" The turtle floated up toward the dolphin to get a better look. "You are a cute little one. What is your name, dear?"

"My name is Nai`a. That is my mother." Nai`a looked quickly behind her to make sure her mother was still there.

"I am pleased to meet you, Nai`a, and happy birthday. I am called Honu," the turtle replied. "I am usually seen in this area. Surely we'll see each other again soon, and thank you for stopping by."

With a nod of the head in reply, Nai`a hurried to catch up with her mother, who had moved ahead.

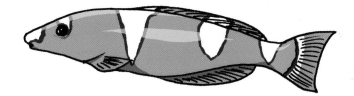

Suddenly there was a very loud and low noise. A sound so strange Nai`a felt fearful. Moving much closer to her mother she looked around quickly, her eyes large with fear.

"What is that sound, mother? Where is it coming from?" There it was again. "WOOOOOOOOO, woooup, woooup, WOOOOOOP, Eeeeeeowwwwoooo."

"Mother! What is that?" Nai`a turned around in several circles, looking in every direction.

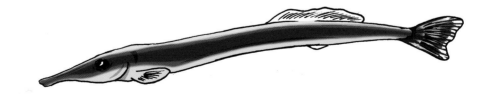

Nai`a and her mother rubbed heads together in a soft caress.

"It's just whales, dear. They sing." Her mother replied.

"They sing? Can we do that? Do you?" Nai`a responded quickly while looking around. She didn't know what a whale was, but was hoping to get to see whoever was making that loud noise.

Her mother chuckled. "No, dear, we don't sing. We make lots of other sounds, though. Like the sounds your auntie makes when she is looking for me, you know, those clicking ones. Also, those calls you make when you want to eat."

Nai`a kept peering into the distance, hoping to see what a whale looked like. "Where are they, mother?"

"Close by, I'm sure. Let's keep going, Nai`a."

As they continued on their journey, Nai`a met an enormous manta ray. She was quick to introduce herself.

"It is very nice to meet you, Nai`a. I am called Hāhālua." He bowed slightly.

"My mother is taking me on a tour. Did you hear that noise earlier? Mother says it is whales singing! Did you know they do that? Why do they sing?"

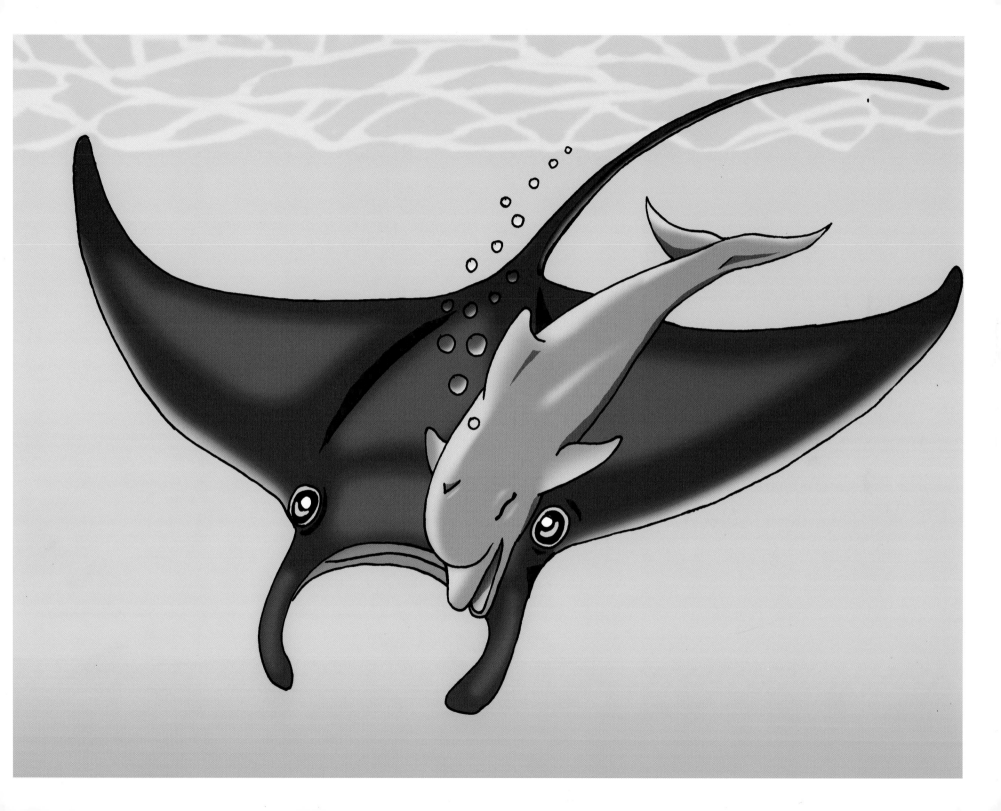

Hāhālua swam upward in a big circle coming down almost beside Naiʻa. "My, you do have lots of questions! Yes, I did hear them, and yes, I do know that. But only the males sing. Most of us think they are talking just to each other, but we don't understand what they say. You don't need to be afraid of them. Do you like it?"

Naiʻa nodded quickly. "Oh yes, I like it very much." Looking upward, she noticed her mother starting to move away. "I have to go now, bye!"

Up ahead Nai'a noticed a large motionless shape. As they got closer she saw a smaller shape, a little larger than her, swimming alongside.

"Mother, who is that? What is that?" she asked excitedly.

"Those are whales, Nai'a. Let's keep going." Her mother started to turn.

"No, wait, please! I want to go see them. Can't we go see them, please?" Nai'a watched the smaller one caress the top of the large whale's head.

"We don't want to bother them, dear. Besides, we still have quite a ways to travel."

"Please, mother. I want to see them. I've never seen anyone so big." Nai'a pleaded.

"Okay, but we won't stay long."

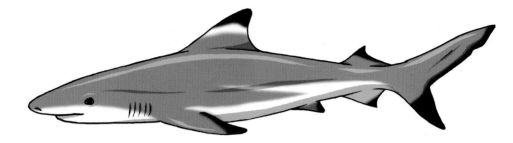

Nai'a and her mother continued up to the very large whale, who appeared to be suspended in the water, barely moving.

"Her eye is closed, mother. Why is her eye closed?" Nai'a asked in a hushed voice.

"I think she is sleeping. Let's go and not bother them." Her mother replied.

"Were they singing earlier?" Nai'a questioned, staring at the whales in wonder. They were so large but she didn't feel afraid anymore.

"No, dear, only the males sing. Remember what Hāhālua said?"

Nai'a nodded, watching the smaller whale, who peered over at her.

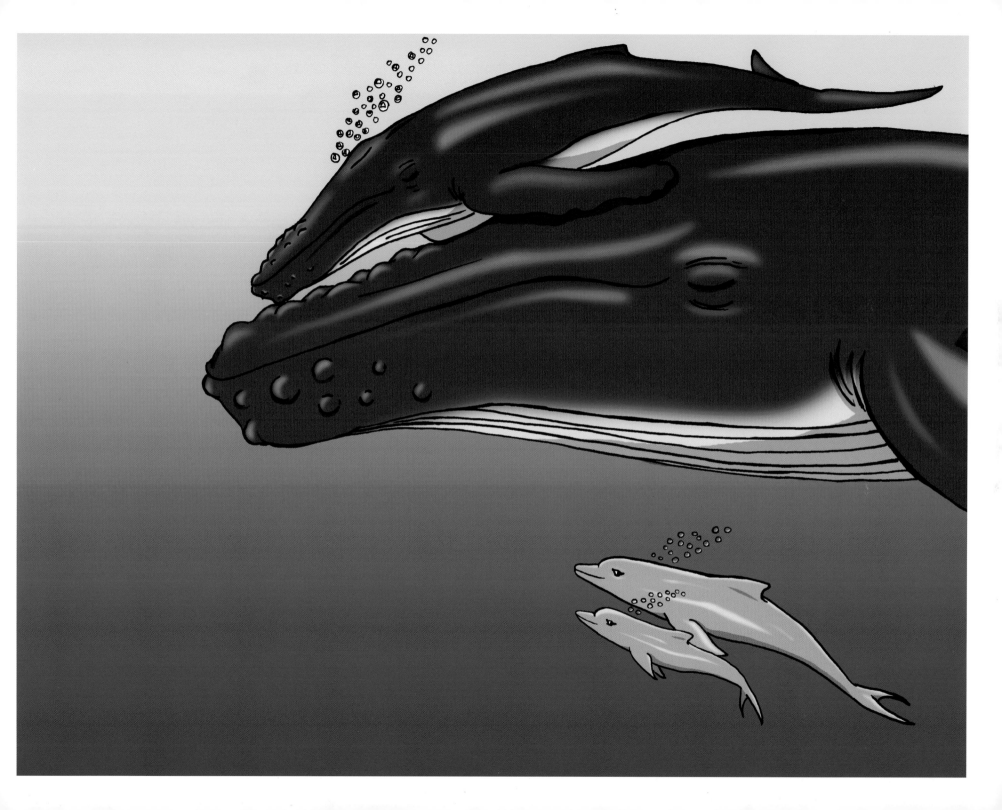

The smaller whale was coming slowly over and looked closely at Nai'a, then smiled sweetly.

"Hello. Who are you? What are you?"

"I am Nai'a. I am a bottlenose dolphin and I live here. Today is my birthday." She looked closely at the small whale. "Who are you?"

"I am Koholā. I am a humpback whale and today is my birthday also! My mom said we are preparing to take a long journey to colder water soon. I will return in a few years, but my mom might come back next year."

Nai'a opened her eyes wide in happy surprise. "Today is your birthday too? That is great! Isn't that wonderful, mother?" She looked at her mother, who was resting now, and turned back to her new friend.

"What are those funny bumps on your head? They're everywhere," she asked while swimming slowly around the whale.

"They are called tubercles. Most of them have hair in them. How come you don't have any?"

Nai'a shook her head. "I don't know. I had hair right on top of my rostrum when I was first born. It is gone now."

The whale came closer to look. "Where did it go?"

Nai'a swam in a quick loop. "I don't know. Hey, look what I can do."

With a few rapid beats of her tail the dolphin jumped out of the water and flipped a loop, entering the water with a soft splash.

"Wow! That was great." The baby whale swam closer to the dolphin and looked at her through large brown eyes. "Hey, how come your rostrum is so long?"

Nai'a shook her head again. "I don't know. How come you don't really have one like mine?"

The whale looked uncertain, then brightened. "I don't know. Let me try what you just did."

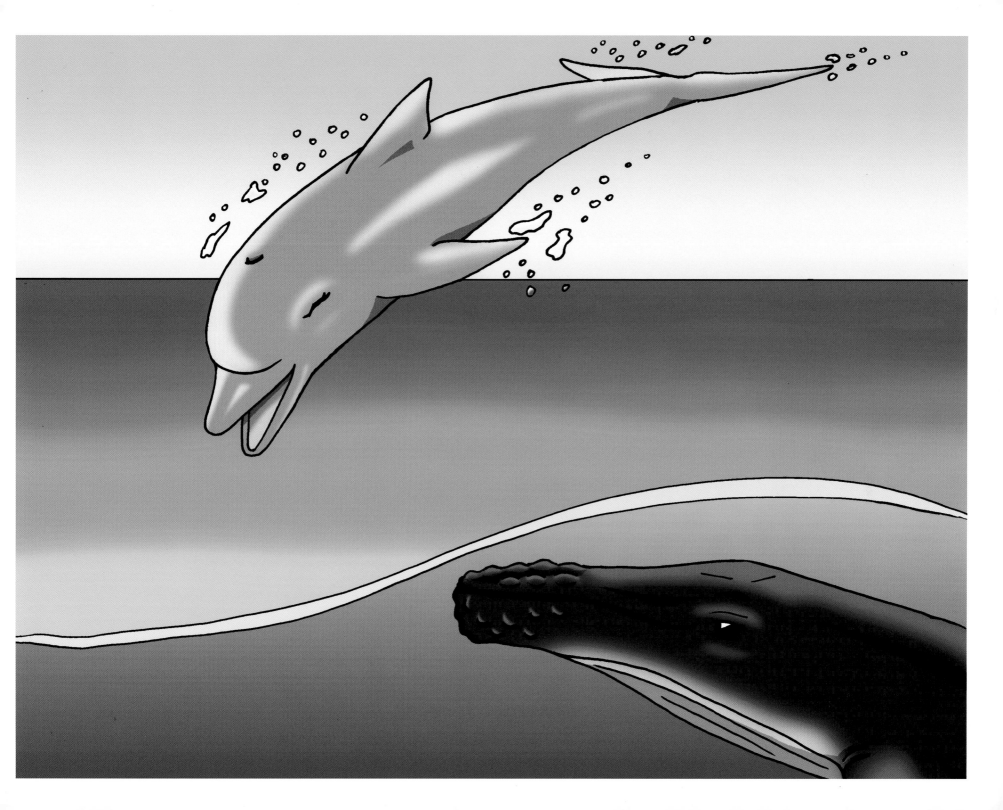

She dove down and turned quickly, arriving at the surface with several beats of her tail. Nai`a was amazed as the whale left the water and turned, landing on her back with a tremendous splash.

"Oh, wow, that was amazing!" Nai'a laughed. "Look at me now!" She swam to the surface and turned her head down, smacking the surface of the water with her tiny tail. Smack, smack, smack, she did it over and over again. Koholā joined her in the fun. Together the two slapped their tails and jumped out of the water over and over. They decided to spend the afternoon playing together and perfecting their moves while their mothers rested.

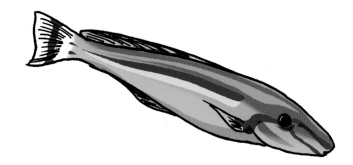

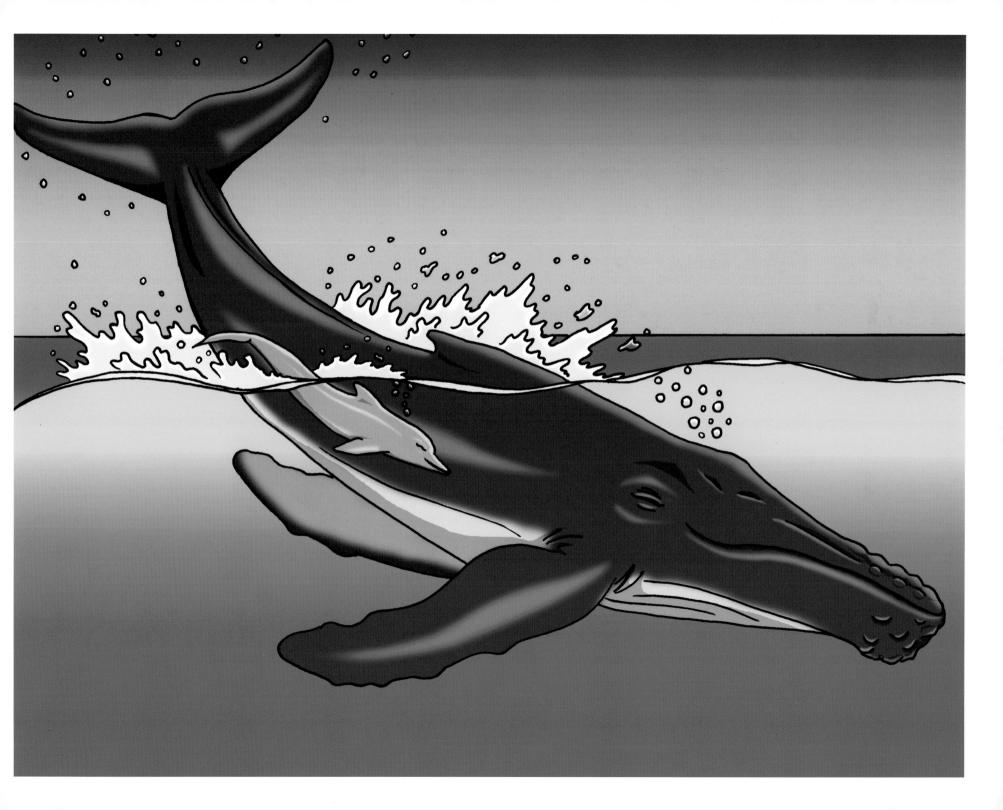

Both the dolphin and the whale learned something very important that day. They learned that it really doesn't matter how different one looks. What matters most is what someone is like on the inside. Both Nai`a and Koholā learned that having a friend is truly valuable. Especially when the friend can be one for a lifetime.

Nai'a's Friends of the Reef

Juvenile Oval Chromis

Lau wiliwili nukunuku 'oi'oi
Longnose Butterflyfish

Hā 'uke'uke kaupali
Helmet Urchin

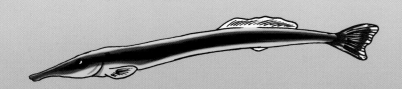

Bluestripe Pipefish

Commerson's Frogfish

Hīnālea lauwili
Saddle Wrasse

Nai'a's Friends of the Reef

'Ālo'ilo'i
Hawaiian Dascyllus

'Iwa
Frigate Bird

Yellow Seahorse

'Ū'ū
Big-scale Soldierfish

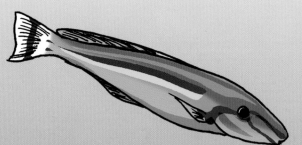

Smalltail Wrasse

Uhu uliuli
Spectacled Parrotfish

Nai'a's Friends of the Reef

Lupe
Broad Stingray

Lauīpala
Yellow Tang

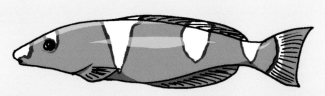

Hīnālea 'akilolo
Juvenile Yellowtail Coris

Mūhe'e
Oval Squid

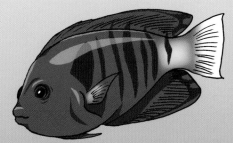

Flame Angelfish

'Ōkole emiemi
Sea Anemone

Nai'a's Friends of the Reef

'Alakuma
Seven Eleven Crab

Hawaiian Cleaner Wrasse

Hailepo
Spotted Eagle Ray

Kūmū
Whitesaddle Goatfish

Aloalo
Mantis Shrimp

Hīnālea 'i'iwi
Bird Wrasse

Nai'a's Friends of the Reef

Humuhumunukunukuāpua'a
Reef Triggerfish

Hōkū kai
Knobby Star

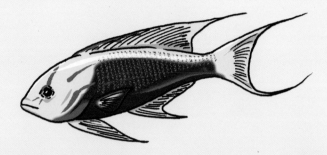

Hawaiian Longfin Anthias

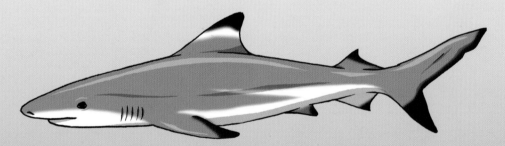

Manō pā'ele
Blacktip Reef Shark

Humuhumu'ele'ele
Black Durgon